First published in the United States and Canada in 2015 by
Lemniscaat USA LLC · New York
Distributed in the United States by Lemniscaat USA LLC · New York

Library of Congress Cataloging-in-Publication Data is available.
ISBN 13: 978-1-935954-48-4 (Hardcover)
Printing and binding: Worzalla, Stevens Point, WI USA
First U.S. edition

Mies van Hout

Pussycat,
Pussycat

Lemniscaat  USA

Five
littleducks
went out one day,

Over the hill and far away.

Mother duck said

Quack, quack, quack, quack,

But only four littleducks

came back.

Down in the meadow
There's an itty bitty pool,
There are three little fishies
And a momma fishy too.

"Swim," said the momma fish,

Swim if you can.

So they swam and they swam

All over the dam.

The elephant goes
This and that.

He's so very big, he's so very fat!

He's got
no fingers, got no toes
But goodness gracious,

What a long nose!

The **itsy**
bitsy
spider

went up the water spout.

Down came the rain and

washed

the spider out!

Out came the sun and dried up all the rain,

And the itsy bitsy spider

went up the spout again.

A **centipede** would certainly need

A hundred stripy socks,

But what will he do when his socks wear through from

climbing trees and rocks?

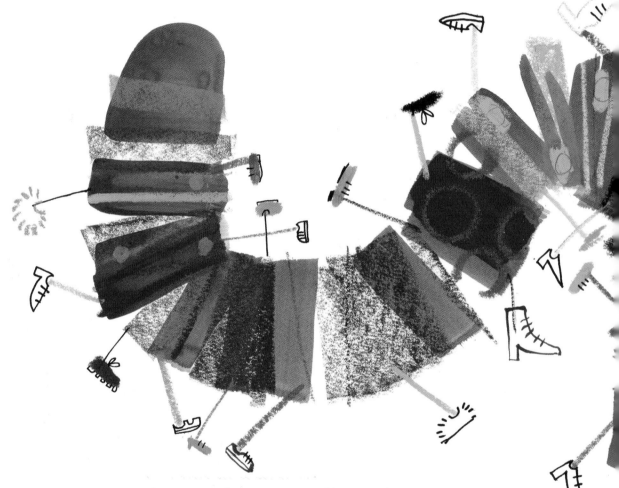

What will he do when his socks wear through,

When all of his socks wear out?

He'll sit in a heap and start to weep, and his

mother begins to shout.

Here's what his mother will shout,

When all of this socks wear out—

I've bought you ten, bought you twenty,

Bought you thirty, forty, fifty,

Bought you sixty, seventy, eighty, ninety,

Bought you a hundred socks!

So off you go, now, sonny,

Do you think I'm made of money?

Until I can afford to buy you more,

You can keep your feet right off the floor!

A wise **old owl**, lived in an oak.

The more he saw, the less he spoke.

The less he spoke,

The more he heard.

Why can't we be,

Like that wise **old bird**?

What can make a
hippopotamus
smile?

What can make him walk for more than a mile?

It's not a party with a paper hat.

Or cake and candy that will make him fat.
That's not what **hippos** do!

They ooze in the gooze without any shoes.
They wade in the water 'til their lips turn blue.
That's what hippos do!

Ride a
cock-horse
to Banbury Cross,

To see a fine lady upon a white horse;

Rings on her fingers and bells on her toes,

And she shall have music wherever she goes.

Pussycat,

pussycat, where have you been?

I've been to London to look at the Queen.
Pussycat, pussycat, what did you there?
I frightened a little mouse under the chair.

Baa,
baa,
black sheep, have you any wool?

Yes sir, yes sir,

three bags full!
One for the master,
One for my dame,
And one for the little boy
Who lives down the lane.

I know a
beetle,
Who lives down a drain.
His coat's very shiny,
But terribly plain.

When I take a
bath,

He comes up the pipe.

Together we wash,

Together we wipe.

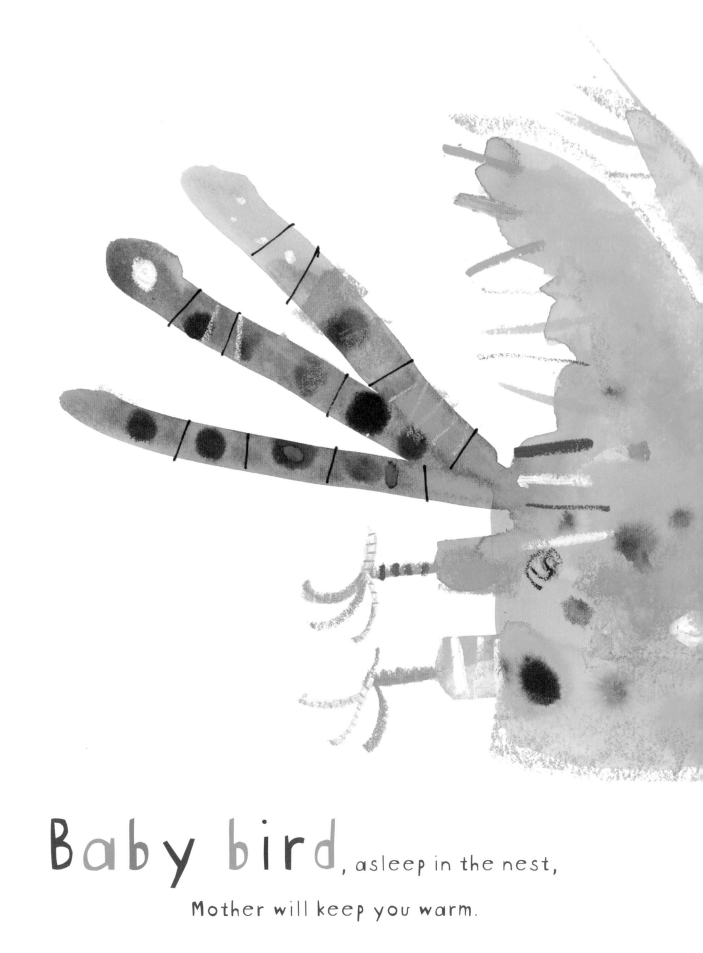

Baby bird, asleep in the nest,

Mother will keep you warm.

Head tucked under feathery wings,

Mother will keep you from harm.